The Littlest Evergreen

Henry Cole

KATHERINE TEGEN BOOKS
An Imprint of HarperCollinsPublishers

Typography by Rachel Zegar
11 12 13 14 15   SCP   10 9 8 7 6 5 4 3 2 1

First Edition

For Marion Dees Miller Faris

I lived on a hillside, with others like me all around.
We grew up together, each year a little more, until
the green tips of our needles nearly touched.

The first spring, I was shorter than the grasses,
shorter than the sparrows! It was tough going for me—
getting enough sunlight—but I dug into the soil, deeper
and deeper, getting stronger and stronger.

Each spring, birds and mice found the hillside. They made their homes in my branches.

On summer days, the heat of the air pulled the pine scent out of my green needles. Afternoons sometimes crackled with lightning and rumbles of thunder. The rain washed away the dust and it felt delicious.

Autumn came. My sap cooled and slowed. Days on the hillside were brisk and short, the nights colder and longer. The cricket songs got slower and slower, fainter and fainter. In winter, I rested under a blanket of snow.

When the titmice and chickadees began to sing, I knew that spring was just a melting snowflake away.

Then one evening in late autumn, a truck came to the hillside. Have you ever had the hairs on your arms stick straight up when a lightning crackle crashes nearby, or when a breeze threatens to fan a brushfire too close? The whine of the chainsaw was like that to me.

We trembled and swayed as the chainsaw blades cut through tree trunks like the wings of a swallow cut through air. Tree after tree slumped over with a soft *whoosh* of needles. Gloved hands grabbed hold of their wounded ends and dropped them onto the back of the truck.

I was one of the lucky ones. "Too small to make much of a tree!" one man said to another. They didn't use the chainsaws on me.

They dug me out of the earth and bound my roots tightly with cloth and rope. Then I, too, was put on the truck.

For the first time ever, I was away from my hillside home. The truck finally stopped. We were dragged off and piled against one another. The sun had come up, but the day was cold. The men huddled around a fire.

Then came other people, hovering like bees around a hive, inspecting us. They touched our branches and smelled our fragrance. A tall man arrived with two children. They pointed and chattered. I was lifted into a car and taken to their home.

It was warm inside the house. The family gave me a drink of cool water, and they hung twinkling strings and bits of glass and metal on my branches.

Later, the house was quiet and dark. Someone came into the room and brought boxes wrapped in bright colors. Soon I was standing among a pile of packages and ribbons.

At daybreak, the children raced into the room, laughing
and shrieking and clawing at the boxes, looking like baby
squirrels as they raced around.

Outside, a winter breeze spotted with snowflakes
swirled around the house. Inside felt hot and stuffy. The
shiny things on my branches got heavier and heavier.

I stood for days and days.

It was a relief when the family came in one morning and
took all the shiny things off.

The tall man lifted me gently again, this time to go outside into the open space. Already a large hole had been dug. There was loose, dark earth at the bottom of the hole. The man cut the twine and bindings and lowered my roots into the coolness of the soil. It felt soft and sweet, and I grabbed hold, never wanting to leave.

The family cared for me for many, many seasons. Year by year the children grew as they played in my lengthening shade. Other friends came too, building their nests.

It's been a long and beautiful life.